The Friendship Cross

S0-AXR-979

William H. Klein
Illustrated by George S. Gaadt
Designed by Frances T. Stewart

BROADMAN
&HOLMAN
PUBLISHERS

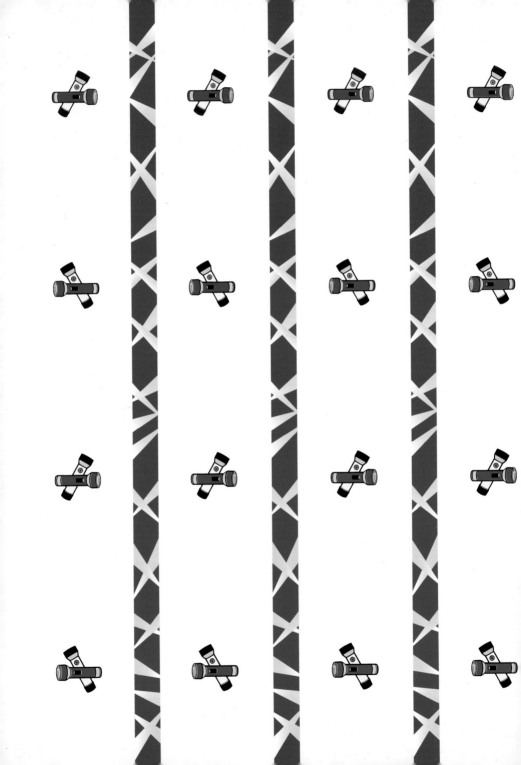

BROADMAN
&HOLMAN
PUBLISHERS

ISBN: 0-8054-1716-8

Dedications

To J.D.D. and J.H.
WHK

To Julia and Rachel
and all best friends everywhere.
FTS

It was an unusually cool Friday afternoon in September when Beth Conklin and Carrie Pippen won the soccer game. Carrie had passed the ball to Beth, who had scored the winning goal.

This did not surprise anyone watching the game, least of all the Conklins and the Pippens, because Carrie and Beth were best friends. Ever since they were six they had celebrated their birthdays together, eaten at each other's house, sat next to each other in school and at church.

At the postgame party the discussion centered on the upcoming election for team captain. Carrie was quite sure that Beth would win. Beth wasn't so sure. In fact, Beth was worried. The newest member of the team had scored the first goal of the game, a girl named Suzie Boyd. "She isn't that popular," Beth thought as she watched Suzie standing quietly by herself in the corner.

What worried Beth was that Suzie was a good soccer player. Beth thought it might be a good thing that Suzie was so shy.

Later that night, while lying in bed after prayers, Carrie saw a flash of light on her wall. It came from Beth's house across the street. She crawled out from under the covers and fumbled under her bed for her flashlight. Once Carrie found it, she flashed it twice out the window, according to their secret code.

With walkie-talkie and flashlight in hand, Carrie peered out her window. "This is Royal Two," she said softly into the microphone.

There was a hiss of static and she heard Beth's radio-filtered voice. "Royal Two, this is Royal One. We had boiled sea slugs for dinner."

Carrie stifled a giggle and thumbed down the send button. "Royal One, this is Royal Two. We had shish kebobbed frogs," said Carrie.

"Royal Two, that is gross," came back Beth.

"And beets," Carrie added, laughing despite herself.

Yuck, that's even grosser!" laughed Beth.

After the giggling stopped, they blinked their flashlights twice, and in familiar unison said, "Good night and God bless."

Carrie closed her eyes and sleepily wondered what sea slugs tasted like.

Beth put away her walkie-talkie in her sock drawer and knelt next to her bed.

"Lord," she prayed, "I want to win the election on Monday, I really do. I hope I win. Bless my mom and dad, and Carrie, and all of my friends. Thank you, Lord. Good night, and watch over me, and if you are not too busy, help me win the election. Please."

Beth climbed into her bed and closed her eyes but couldn't go to sleep. Instead, she thought about the election and about Suzie Boyd.

Sunday, after church, Beth and Carrie ate lunch on the Pippen's back porch.

"Carrie, I'm worried about the election for team captain," said Beth nervously.

Carrie chuckled as she sipped her milk. "You should be. A top soccer player should know that eating sea slugs makes you run slower."

Beth sighed. "Carrie, I'm serious."

Carrie instantly sobered. "What is it, Beth?"

"It's that new girl. What if she wins?" asked Beth worriedly.

"Oh, Beth. Suzie Boyd? Why would she win?" asked Carrie around a mouthful of peanut butter and jelly.

"She's such a good soccer player. I'm not that good," answered Beth.

People don't know her as well as you. Besides, she seems so shy," replied Carrie.

"Yeah, I guess she is. She is shy," stated Beth.

"Well, she's new. She'll get over it," said Carrie, wondering to herself if Suzie would win the election on Monday.

"Maybe she's hiding something," said Beth.

"Like what?" asked Carrie.

"I don't know. Maybe she's a cheater."

Carrie chuckled. "Maybe she eats boiled sea slugs."

When Carrie arrived at school Monday morning, she heard a terrible thing.

"Carrie!" said Tina Hefflin excitedly. "Did you hear? Suzie Boyd was kicked off her last soccer team for lying about her age! Once, she even got a red card!" In the distance, Carrie could see Beth whispering to two of their soccer teammates.

Carrie moved down the hall in a daze and she felt a horrible sinking feeling in the pit of her stomach.

"Morning, Carrie," said Beth warmly. "Did you hear? Suzie Boyd seems to have a dark secret."

Carrie looked at her best friend and felt like crying. "Where did you hear this, Beth?" she asked quietly.

Beth glanced around quickly to make sure no one was nearby. "I made it up."

"Oh Beth, why?" asked Carrie, her voice cracking.

"I'm winning the election, Carrie," said Beth. "No one will vote for Suzie now. She's a cheater."

"You're the one who's cheating, Beth," said Carrie as the tears began to flow down her cheeks.

Beth looked at her a moment, and chewed thoughtfully on her bottom lip. "You aren't planning to tell on me, are you?"

"Beth… you lied!" Carrie turned on her heel and ran down the hallway, toward the principal's office.

"Carrie Pippen! Don't you dare! You're my best friend! You can't!"

But it was too late.

The aftermath had been brutally swift and painful. Beth was grounded for a month, her best friend had betrayed her, and Suzie Boyd was the new captain of the soccer team. Her parents were still discussing with Coach Hefflin how long their daughter should be suspended from the team. Beth barely ate, slept poorly, and most of all, she ignored the two flashes of light from the house across the street.

Although Carrie walked with Tina and other classmates to school, she never gave up hope that Beth would join them. Beth would watch out the window until Carrie and the others had gone on before walking to school alone.

$\mathcal{S}$unday morning, Beth woke up early. She'd awakened every day since Monday feeling miserable, and alone.

"I would have won," sobbed Beth into her pillow. "And I lost all my friends… and Carrie, she told on me!"

Every day, all of the other children kept their distance from Beth. She was a liar. She was an outcast. Everyone ignored her, except for Carrie. Every day Carrie tried to approach Beth, at the cafeteria, during recess, and on the walk home. Every day Beth had ignored her. Beth just couldn't see why Carrie would try to remain friends. It was Carrie's fault, all of it.

In church, Beth and her parents always sat in the seventh row. That next Sunday, Carrie and her family were in the fourth row. All through the service Carrie could feel Beth's eyes burning into the back of her head.

Reverend Heath was giving the sermon. "As we learned from the gospel reading of Matthew, Jesus was left alone, in the Garden of Gethsemane. He had taken three disciples with him: Peter and the two sons of Zebedee, whom he left behind while he went farther into the garden to pray, alone.

When Jesus finished praying, he returned to the three disciples and found them sleeping. They had not stayed awake with him, even for an hour, while he prayed. Although Jesus' disciples followed and admired him, he was left to face his fate alone in the end. And he did."

$\mathcal{C}$arrie listened closely to every word of the sermon. After the service, she carefully waited to be the last one to be greeted by Reverend Heath. "Hello, Carrie, how are you?"

In a moment, all of Carrie's feelings began to rush out of her. They sat together in the pew, as Carrie explained everything that had happened between Beth and her.

"Jesus and God are always with us, even when we're all alone, right Reverend Heath?" Carrie asked him tentatively.

Reverend Heath smiled. "Our savior did not die upon the cross with bitterness towards fellow man, Carrie, he died with love in his heart, and with understanding and forgiveness."

Do you think God can help me get through to Beth, to show her that I'm still her friend?" asked Carrie.

"Yes I do, Carrie. I think that God can always help us, if we let Him," said Reverend Heath.

"But how?" Carrie asked. Just then, she caught herself reaching for her necklace. It was a small gold cross, given to her by her Grandfather Jack.

Just as Reverend Heath began to answer, Carrie smiled. "I think I know," she said. "Thank you, Sir."

Carrie ran from the church, excitement giving her speed.

Beth was in her room when the doorbell rang. She told her parents she was doing homework, but she really wanted to think in private. Her mind kept returning to Reverend Heath's sermon. How lonely Jesus must have been! So many people loved him, yet he was abandoned and betrayed by them. Beth began to cry, and knelt beside her bed.

"Oh God, I know I didn't do the right thing. I really messed up. I lied so that I'd win. But I lost. I lost everything, and most of all my best friend! I'm so sorry… I wish I could take it back… but I can't. Jesus, I have not been true to you or to my friend. Can you forgive me?"

At that moment, there was a soft knock at her bedroom door. Beth stood quickly, wiping away her tears, and opened the door.

Beth, someone left this on the front step," Mrs. Conklin said as she stood in the doorway, smiling sadly.

It was a small cardboard box with Beth's name written on it. Beth's heart started to pound faster when she recognized the handwriting.

"May I open this alone, please?" asked Beth timidly.

"Of course." As Beth's mother eased the door shut, Beth opened the box.

Inside the box was a note, which read: "In God's love, your best friend, Carrie."

And below the note was a symbol of love and forgiveness, the gold necklace, which her friend Carrie always wore.

Just as Carrie reached her front porch, she heard a familiar voice.

"Carrie!" Beth shouted.

Carrie could see Beth running across the street, her face wet and red, something shining in her right hand. Carrie knew what it was.

In moments they embraced, both crying, as Beth tried to press the beautiful, tiny cross back into Carrie's hand.

"But it was a special gift to you from your grandfather. I couldn't!" said Beth.

"No," whispered Carrie softly, "it's a special gift to all of us, from God."

Beth's eyes shone as Carrie fastened the thin chain around her best friend's neck.

"I'm so sorry," Beth whispered, hugging Carrie tightly. "I'm so sorry. I was so wrong. You are my best friend, Carrie. I really missed you."

"I missed you, too," sighed Carrie, and then she paused, giving Beth a questioning look.

"What is it?" asked Beth.

"Do you think we can ask your parents to 'unground' you long enough to come for dinner? We have a lot of catching up to do," added Carrie.

"Yeah," sniffed Beth. "But no sea slugs, okay?"

"Nope. Just beets."

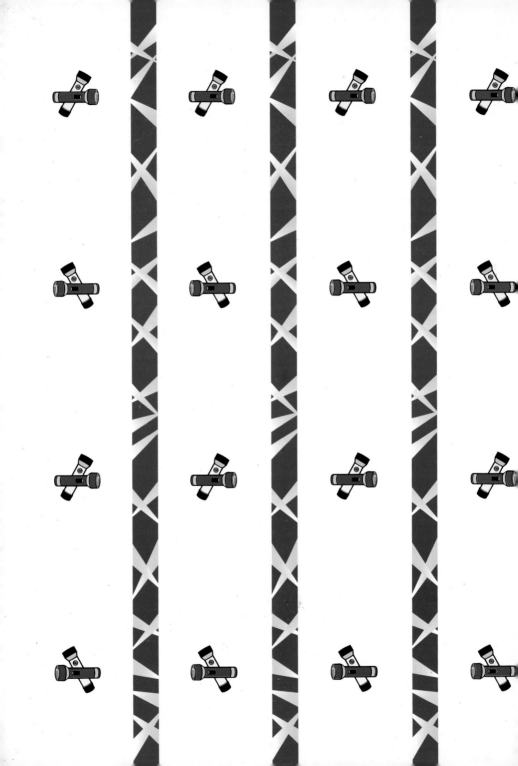